For my friend,
Estelle

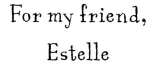
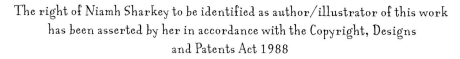
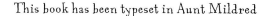
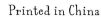
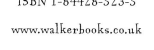

First published 2004 by Walker Books Ltd
87 Vauxhall Walk, London SE11 5HJ

This edition published 2005

2 4 6 8 10 9 7 5 3

© 2004 Niamh Sharkey

The right of Niamh Sharkey to be identified as author/illustrator of this work
has been asserted by her in accordance with the Copyright, Designs
and Patents Act 1988

This book has been typeset in Aunt Mildred

Printed in China

British Library Cataloguing in Publication Data:
a catalogue record for this book is available from the British Library

ISBN 1-84428-523-5

www.walkerbooks.co.uk

THIS WALKER BOOK BELONGS TO:

_____

_____

_____

Santasaurus

Niamh Sharkey

WALKER BOOKS
AND SUBSIDIARIES
LONDON · BOSTON · SYDNEY · AUCKLAND

W

hen the snow began to fall before Christmas,

Ollie, Molly and Milo wrote letters

to Santasaurus.

Ollie wished for

a dinobot.

Molly wished for a dinocycle.

All Milo wanted was to meet

Santasaurus and to fly

in his sleigh.

When the cold wind blew

through Dinosaur Town,

Ollie, Molly and Milo went

Christmas shopping with Mumosaurus.

"What hustle and bustle and squoosh!"

said Mumosaurus.

Later, Mumosaurus, Dadosaurus,
Ollie, Molly and Milo
wrapped up presents
in fancy paper,

hung up
paperchains,

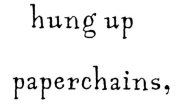

turned on

the fairy lights,

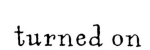

made popcorn strings to hang on the tree

and baked sugar-plum cakes

for everyone.

It's Christmas Eve!

Everything is ready for the Dinosaurs' Christmas.
Ollie, Molly and Milo hang up their stockings,
leave milk and cookies for Santasaurus
and carrots for the dinodeer.

Soon everyone
is sleeping ...

except Milo.

Listen! What's that?
Is it the sound of
sleigh-bells ringing?

Milo pops out

from under the covers and

creeps ever so quietly down the stairs.

Who is standing by the Christmas tree?

SANTASAURUS!

"Ho ho ho, Milo! I was waiting for you."

In the blink of a magic eye,

Milo and Santasaurus

shot up the chimney

to the sleigh on the roof.

They flew up from the house ...

and over Dinosaur Town.

They delivered presents to dinosaur children

all over Dinosaur World.

It was still dark when Santasaurus
brought Milo home.

"Goodnight, dinodeer!" Milo said,
giving each one a carrot.

"Goodnight, Santasaurus,
and thank you for the sleigh ride!"

Milo was back in bed and
fast asleep before you could say
"plum pudding".

"Hurray!" shouted Molly.
"It's Christmas morning!"

Ollie's best present
was a cool dinobot!

Molly got

a smashing dinocycle!

And Milo?

Milo got a miniature sleigh,

eight little dinodeer and a Christmas hat

just like the one Santasaurus wore!

So, were all the dinosaurs happy?
Yesosaurus, they were!
Happy Christmas,
Ollie, Molly and Milo!

Happy Christmas,
Mumosaurus and Dadosaurus!
HAPPY DINOSAURS' CHRISTMAS!

WALKER BOOKS is the world's leading
independent publisher of children's books.
Working with the best authors and illustrators
we create books for all ages, from babies
to teenagers – books your child will
grow up with and always remember. So…

FOR THE BEST CHILDREN'S BOOKS,
LOOK FOR THE BEAR